# Disappointed, But Not Too Disappointed

*Dave Jackson*

Illustrated by Susan Lexa

**Chariot Books**
DAVID C. COOK PUBLISHING CO.

*Dedicated to*
*Nicholas and Brad*

Chariot Books is an imprint of David C. Cook Publishing Co.
David C. Cook Publishing Co., Elgin, Illinois 60120
David C. Cook Publishing Co., Weston, Ontario

DISAPPOINTED, BUT NOT TOO DISAPPOINTED
© 1987 by Dave Jackson for the text and Susan Lexa for the illustrations.

First printing, 1987
Printed in the United States of America
91 90 89 88 87      5 4 3 2 1

Library of Congress
Cataloging-in-Publication Data

Jackson, Dave.
   Disappointed, but not too disappointed.

   (Storybooks for caring parents)
   Summary: Stories with accompanying Scripture quotations suggest ways of dealing with disappointments such as being prevented by illness from attending the first day of school, having unfulfilled expectations, and attempting and failing to care for a pet fish.
   1. Disappointment—Juvenile literature. 2. Christian life—1960—Juvenile literature.
[1. Disappointment. 2. Conduct of life. 3. Christian life] I. Lexa, Susan, ill. II. Title. III. Series.
BF575.D57J33 1987    155.4'24    86-2602
ISBN 0-89191-298-3

Scripture references identified (NIV) are from the New International Version; those identified (TEV) are from Today's English Version.

# Contents

# For Parents

When I was a small child, my grandmother's house seemed like a castle. The living room was a great hall with a fireplace at one end and a heavy wrought iron chandelier hanging from a lofted, beamed ceiling. The hallway leading to the back bedrooms was so long that I got tired running back and forth (when I wasn't stopped and told to walk in the house). Then my family moved far away for a few years and I grew several inches taller. What a surprise to return and find how grandmother's house had shrunk.

As adults we often have a hard time remembering how big things seemed when we were little. Disappointments which seem small to us can be huge to a child who hasn't grown accustomed to having plans changed, special items broken, hopes go unrealized.

But in addition to lacking the experience to know that most disappointments can be survived, there's another reason why disappointments loom so large for children. Most disappointments are related to time. We wait (time) for something to happen. But time for children is much different than it is for adults. Time is only comprehended in relative terms. For a six-year-old, a year may be a full third of his or her conscious experience. Imagine waiting eight or more years (a third of your life experience) for something as important to you as starting school is for a child. This is why, the older we get, the faster "time flies." As an adult, there are few things in your life you wait for as relatively long as children wait for most things.

This Storybook for Caring Parents emphasizes three specific ways we as parents can help our children cope with disappointments.

## Express Empathy

*The Mumps* is about Jeffrey's great disappointment in not getting to attend school on opening day because of a case of mumps. Jeffrey's greatest need at this time of disappointment is to know that someone truly understands how he feels. His dad is able to respond by sharing a personal

experience which assures Jeffrey that he really does understand.

You may not be able to respond to your child's disappointments with as dramatic a parallel, but that's not important. (In fact, it's not desirable to always claim you've "had the same experience.") The important thing is to communicate to your child that he or she is living in the same world in which you live, and most important, the same world Jesus lived in. And therefore Jesus, you, and other people *can* understand and *do* care.

## Alternatives Help

*Smashed Hopes* suggests another important way to deal with disappointments. When our expectations go unfulfilled, God has something else (often better) for us. Sometimes we can't see this immediately. Nevertheless, it is an occasion to redirect our attention.

When your children experience disappointment, you shouldn't feel obliged to compensate them with a replacement. Life isn't like that, and that's not what God means when he promises that "all things work together for good" (Romans 8:28).

However, redirecting our attention to alternatives can help us understand God's plan in a new way.

This story suggests another aspect of God's purpose when we face troubles. Sometimes God allows disappointments to draw us closer to him and to one another. Jeffrey's sister is the one who gives the first hint of a helpful alternative, and Jeffrey's father helps him follow through in a satisfying way.

## What Can Be Learned?

*Belly Up* is about Jeffrey's disappointment when he attempts and fails to care for an angelfish.

Most of us encourage or allow our children to attempt things that are beyond them. That's good if it's not too much beyond them, and if we protect them from a diet of failure. Trying new things (which involves the potential of failure) is how they learn. But any failure needs to be accompanied by positive learning.

Jeffrey fails partially because he is too young for the responsibility and partly because he (and his mother) don't know *how* to care for the angelfish. Being more responsible and getting some facts about *how* to care for angelfish are the lessons Jeffrey learns.

4

# The Mumps

J effrey punched the pillow on the sofa, sat up, and took a sip from his juice glass. "Mom, will first grade be like kindergarten?" he called.

"In some ways yes; in some ways no," she said, coming into the room with a bowl in her hands.

"How is it different?" Jeff asked.

"Well, you'll stay at school longer each day. You'll come home with your sister. And you'll start learning more. . . ."

"Will I be able to read?" he asked excitedly.

"In time."

"I already know all my letters and numbers. I can't wait," Jeffrey said.

"Monday will come soon enough. It's only two days away. But first you have to get over your sore throat," Mom added, with a worried look on her face. "This afternoon I'm taking you to the doctor."

"I don't want to go to the doctor. He'll give me pills or maybe even a shot. Besides, it's my neck, not my throat. Right here on each side below my ears."

When Jeffrey was examined that afternoon, the

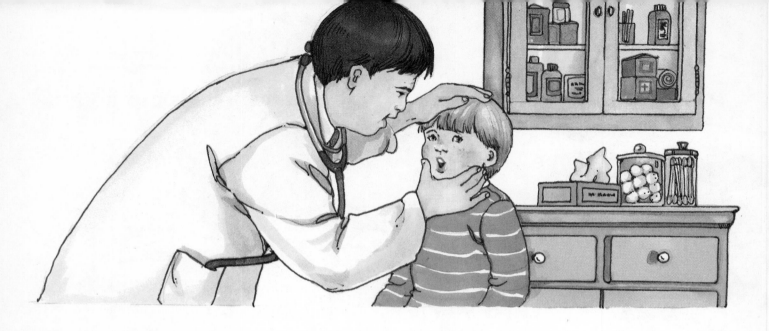

doctor stood back and said, "Well, young man, I'm afraid you have the mumps."

Jeffrey looked anxiously at Mom and then at the doctor. "Will I be well for school?"

"By Monday? Hardly," said the doctor. "You should be *feeling* better by then, but you won't be ready to go to school for a week or more."

Jeffrey didn't say anything as he walked out of the office with Mom, but in the car he began to cry. "Mom, I want to go to school. I'll even take a pill."

"I'll give you aspirin to help you feel better, Jeff, but you'll still have to stay home and rest."

"But, Mom, you don't understand. I've *got* to go to school. It's the first day."

At home Jeffrey sat on the sofa, looking out the window and waiting for Dad to come home. Maybe he would understand. Pretty soon he saw Dad far away, coming down the sidewalk. Jeffrey could always recognize his dad's walk even before he could see his face. That was because Dad had a funny bounce Mom called a limp.

"Dad, I've *got* to go to school the first day," Jeffrey said, after Mom explained about the mumps. "If I dont't, all the other kids will become friends, but I won't know anyone."

"I wish you could," said Dad, "but you've got to get well first. I'm sure you're very disappointed. I know just how you feel."

"No, you don't!" shouted Jeffrey. "Nobody knows, not you or anyone."

"Well, maybe not," said Dad. "But tonight, instead of reading a story, I'm going to *tell* you a story about another little boy who was very disappointed one time when *he* got sick."

At bedtime, Jeffrey was still very upset and disappointed, but he was glad to hear a story.

"Once upon a time," started Dad, "there was a boy about three years older than you, and he loved to play baseball. He was pretty good, too—the best center fielder on his Little League team. But just before the opening game of the season, he got sick.

"Of course, he missed the game. In fact, he was so sick that he had to go to the hospital. He stayed there for days . . . and weeks."

"Did he have mumps?" asked Jeffrey.

"Oh, no. Mumps last only a few days. This boy had a disease called polio. Now there's medicine so children won't get it. Anyway, he was in the hospital for almost a year and had a very painful operation to help him walk again. Even then one foot didn't work quite right. When he got well, he played baseball for fun whenever he could, but he never got to be on a real team again. His limp kept him from running fast the way he did before.

"What do you think, Jeff? Was that little boy as disappointed as you are?"

"Sure," nodded Jeffrey. "*He* would know just how I feel."

"Well, Jeff," said Dad, and his voice got very quiet, "I was that little boy who didn't get to play in the opening game."

Jeff sat silently; then he threw his arms around Dad. They hugged each other for a long time.

"Dad," Jeffrey said, "now I *know* you understand." ∎

# From God's Word

. . . God has said,
  "Never will I leave you;
  never will I forsake you."
So we say with confidence,
  "The Lord is my helper."
—*Hebrews 13:5, 6 (NIV)*

# Think It Through

Ask your children these questions and discuss the answers.

1. What was Jeffrey looking forward to?

2. Why did Jeffrey think he needed to be at school on the first day?

3. Why did Jeffrey's dad know just how Jeffrey felt?

4. Describe how you felt when you were very disappointed about something and didn't think anyone understood.

5. Even if your parents don't seem to understand, Who knows for sure just how you feel when you are disappointed?

# Story 2 | Smashed Hopes

Every day Jeffrey and his older sister, Lois, ran to the door when the mail came so that they could get it before Mom saw it.

Four weeks earlier they had made ink drawings on special plastic and sent them away to a company that would transfer the drawings to fancy dinner plates. Those plates were going to be Mom's birthday present. But her birthday was just two days away, and the plates still hadn't come.

Jeffrey had worked very hard on his picture of a clown. He knew Mom loved clowns, because once he had made a picture of one at school by pasting brightly colored pieces of felt together, and Mom always said it was her favorite. It hung over Jeffrey's bed. He had carefully copied it for the plate, drawing an ink picture that looked just like the felt clown.

" 'Allow three to four weeks for delivery,' " Dad had read as he helped them send off the drawings. "That's cutting it close, but they should make it."

Suddenly their dog, Tippy, started barking. "That must be the mail carrier," said Lois, as she jumped up and ran for the door.

Jeffrey followed close behind and got to the door

just as the mail carrier handed Lois a small brown package. It was just the right size to hold the plates.

"Here," said Lois, as she stuffed a few letters toward Jeffrey. "You take these to Mom before she comes out, and I'll run upstairs with the plates."

Jeffrey pulled back. "No. You take the letters, and let me have the package."

"Come on," said Lois. "I got it first."

"Well, don't open it until I get there," he said as he grabbed the letters and ran to give them to Mom.

But when he got upstairs, Lois was working on the package with a pair of scissors. "I *said*, don't open it until I got here."

"It's not open," said Lois. "I only cut the tape."

Soon the package was open, and there was Lois's drawing of a fat bird sitting on a branch—but it looked so much fancier. It was almost like magic to see it part of a beautiful, shiny plate.

Jeffrey grabbed the box and pulled back the packing paper, looking for his plate underneath. But

all he found was a letter and another piece of plastic.

"Where's my plate?" he wailed. "How come my plate's not here?"

Lois looked up from admiring her plate. "They probably shipped it in a separate package. It'll come tomorrow."

"But what if it doesn't?"

"Don't worry," she said as she grabbed the packing box. "Here's a letter. I bet it says your plate will come tomorrow." But when she read it, it said, " 'Dear Customer: We are sorry to inform you that

18

your drawing was accidentally destroyed in the transfer process. Therefore, we are enclosing a second plastic for you to try again. Return this letter with your new drawing and there will be no charge.' "

"They ruined it," said Jeffrey in a whisper. "They ruined my drawing. What will I give Mom for her birthday?"

There wasn't time to make another drawing and get a plate back. That would take four more weeks.

"Why don't you give her something else?"

suggested Lois.

But what could it be? Nothing was as nice as the plate that Lois was going to give. Why, it was almost as beautiful as his felt clown picture.

Suddenly Jeffrey had an idea. The felt clown picture, the one that Mom loved so much—he could give it to her.

When Dad got home, Jeffrey told him what had happened.

"I'm really sorry about the plate," said Dad, "but I think giving the felt picture is a great idea."

"But I wish it were new, Dad. She won't be surprised."

"What if I helped you make a nice frame for it?"

"That would do it. That would make it special."

Late that evening, when the clown picture was in its shiny new frame, and he and Dad were wrapping it, Jeffrey still felt disappointed that he couldn't give a plate. But he knew Mom would be happy with this present, too. ∎

# From God's Word

People may plan all kinds of things, but the Lord's will is going to be done.

—*Proverbs 19:21 (TEV)*

# Think It Through

Ask your children these questions and discuss the answers.

1. Why did Jeffrey and Lois want to get the mail before their mom got it each day?

2. How do you think Jeffrey felt when he learned his plate had been destroyed? Tell about a time when you have felt the same way.

3. Why couldn't Jeffrey just make a new ink drawing for a new plate?

4. Jeffrey thought of a different gift to give his mom. How can alternatives (second choices) help someone get over a disappointment?

# Belly Up

M om, may I *please* have an angelfish? I'll take good care of it," begged Jeffrey.

"I'm not sure. An angelfish is harder to take care of than a goldfish. Angelfish are tropical fish, and they are more delicate."

"But I take good care of my goldfish, don't I?"

"Well, for six years old you do pretty well. But sometimes you forget to feed them, and sometimes you let the water get dirty without cleaning it."

"But I won't with the angelfish. Please. They only cost two dollars for the little ones at the pet store, and I could use the money that I've saved."

"You really want one enough to use your own money?" asked Mom.

"Yeah. And I've been saving my allowance for a long time."

"Well, I guess you can, but I don't think it's a very good idea. There may be a lot of special things you have to know about caring for an angelfish."

"Oh, no. Bill's big brother has a fish tank with lots of angelfish. It's not hard to care for them. Sometimes Bill even feeds them."

That afternoon Jeffrey and Mom did errands. On the way home they stopped at the pet shop and Jeffrey bought the prettiest little angelfish in the tank—bright silver with black stripes. At home he

put it in the fishbowl with his two goldfish.

"Come look," Jeffrey called to his sister, Lois.

"That's great," said Lois. "But the water looks dirty to me. Why don't you change it?"

"Okay," said Jeffrey. He carefully picked up the heavy bowl and carried it to the bathroom. He adjusted the water in the bathtub so it was running a slow stream that wasn't too cold. Then he set the bowl under the stream in the tub and let it fill to overflowing. He had found that if the water ran very slowly, it could overflow without his goldfish swimming out. In a while the water would be nice and clean. Then he would pour out the extra and carry the bowl back to his room. But before he finished, the doorbell rang.

"Jeffrey, Billy is here," Lois called.

Jeffrey ran out of the bathroom to meet his friend at the front door. "Hey, Billy, guess what? I got an angelfish."

"Yeah? That's neat. Know what I did yesterday?

My Uncle Scott came to visit, and he gave me a ride
in his airplane. We flew right over here, and I could
see my house and your house and the whole street!"

Jeffrey wished he could have flown. The boys
went outside and played airplane, running around
the yard with their arms out like wings. Half an hour
later, Jeffrey suddenly remembered.

"My fish!" he cried, running into the house.
When he got to the bathroom, he saw a sad sight.

His new angelfish was flat on its side in the
fishbowl, going round and round as the water

poured in. The goldfish looked okay, but not the angelfish. Jeffrey reached down to touch it. It didn't move, and he noticed that the water was ice cold. While he was outside, the temperature had changed.

"Mom, Mom! Come quick," Jeffrey cried.

Both Mom and Billy came running.

"What's the matter?" asked Mom.

"My angelfish is sick. Can you fix it?"

Billy looked into the tub. "It's not sick," he said. "It's belly up."

"What's that mean?"

"It means it's dead. You can't keep an angelfish in a little fishbowl. My brother's fish have special water and a heater and everything."

Pretty soon Billy went home, and Mom helped Jeffrey bury the angelfish outside in the flower garden. She held him while he cried a little.

"I know you really wanted that fish," said Mom. "You used money you had saved for a long time."

Later, when they went into the house, Mom

said, "I wonder, Jeffrey . . . what do you think we can learn from this situation?"

"I don't know," said Jeffrey.

"Well, think a minute."

"I shouldn't have gone off and left the water running, because it had to stay warm."

"Yes, that's one thing. But, as Billy said, I think there is a lot more about angelfish we need to learn before we try to have one again. Maybe they can tell us at the pet store."

"Yeah. Or maybe Billy's brother can teach us."

"Maybe he can." ■

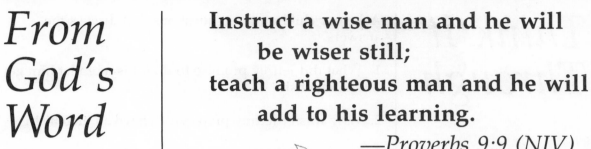

# From God's Word

**Instruct a wise man and he will be wiser still; teach a righteous man and he will add to his learning.**

*—Proverbs 9:9 (NIV)*

# Think It Through

Ask your children these questions and discuss the answers.

1. What did Jeffrey promise to do if his mom let him get an angelfish?

2. Why wasn't Jeffrey prepared to have an angelfish?

3. What did Jeffrey's mom suggest they do as a result of his great disappointment when the angelfish died?

4. Describe a disappointing situation you have had. What did you learn from it?